Disney

MICKEY MOUSE

The Scariest Halloween Story Ever!

P9-DCL-472

Read-Along

STORYBOOK AND CD

Mickey Mouse tries to tell scary Halloween stories to his nephews, but can he make them *spooky* enough? Find out as you read along with me in your book. You will know it is time to turn the page when you hear this chilling sound. . . . Let's begin now.

Copyright © 2018 Disney Enterprises, Inc. All rights reserved. Published by Disney Press, an imprint of Disney Book Group. No part of this book may be reproduced or transmitted in any form or by any means, electronic or mechanical, including photocopying, recording, or by any information storage and retrieval system, without written permission from the publisher. For information address Disney Press, 1200 Grand Central Avenue, Glendale, California 91201.

Printed in the United States of America

First Paperback Edition, July 2018

3 5 7 9 10 8 6 4 2

ISBN 978-1-368-02052-7
FAC-028327-19091

For more Disney Press fun, visit www.disneybooks.com

SUSTAINABLE FORESTRY INITIATIVE
Certified Sourcing
www.sfiprogram.org
SFI-00993
Logo Applies to Text Stock Only

DISNEY PRESS

Los Angeles • New York

It was Halloween night, and the town was alive! Mickey, Donald, their nephews, and Goofy were dressed up and excited to trick-or-treat.

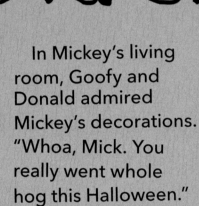

They got their fair share of candy and returned to Mickey's decked-out house. "**Trick or treat**, smell my feet, gimme something good to eat."

In Mickey's living room, Goofy and Donald admired Mickey's decorations. "Whoa, Mick. You really went whole hog this Halloween."

"Just you wait. I still have one more **surprise** in store!"

Mickey turned to his nephews, who devoured their pile of candy like goblins. "Okay, Huey, Dewey, Louie, Morty, Ferdie, who's ready for the perfect treat to top off this spooktacular Halloween?"

 "Oh, what is it, Uncle Mickey?"

Mickey grew very serious and theatrical. "The ultimate scary story."

"Yay! Scary story! Scary story! Scary story!"

Goofy, Donald, and the nephews gathered around, eager to hear Mickey's story. Mickey dramatically switched off the lights, drew the curtains, and cleared the furniture.

"Scoot in closer. *Ahem* . . . Before we begin, it would be unkind to present this tale without just a word of friendly **warning**.

It's one of the **strangest** stories ever told. It might . . . **shock** you! It might even . . . **horrify** you!"

Mickey paused for effect. "It was a dark, stormy night . . . .

"Something **strange** was afoot in the castle of Dr. Victor Goofenstein."

In the doctor's laboratory, Dr. Victor Goofenstein and Duckor the hunchback created . . . a scary **monster**!

"It lives! A-ha-ha-ha! It lives!"

Only the monster wasn't scary at all. In fact, it had the happy head of . . . Mickey!

"Golly, **I'm alive**! And I'm lovin' it!"

Mickey's nephews weren't spooked in the slightest. They wanted a truly **scary** story, as promised.

Mickey realized he had to do better to frighten them. "Okay, you guys want a *really* scary story, huh? Just remember, you *asked* for it. Long ago, in a time of **darkness** . . ." Mickey continued to tell his audience about a great vampire hunter named **Van Mousing** and his trustworthy companions.

The group made it inside a vampire's castle, where the **vampire** trapped them and attacked!

Luckily, Van Mousing yanked open the curtains, allowing sunlight to **burn** the vampire to ashes.

"The hunters celebrated, but all was not well. For during the heat of battle, Van Mousing had been bitten. The vampire hunter became . . .

". . . a vampire."

"Nobody saw that coming!"

"We *all* saw it coming!" The nephews still weren't impressed by Mickey's candy corn fangs.

"That wasn't scary at all!"

Mickey disagreed. "You guys are nuts! **That was super scary!**"

The nephews pelted Mickey with **eggs** and **tomatoes**.

Feeling defeated, Mickey ran into the kitchen, looking to his friends for what to do.

"Face it, Mick. You come from the *happiest* place on earth. You're just not capable of telling a scary story."

Mickey sank to the floor. "I guess you're right. There is no way I can tell a scary story. I better get out there and tell the boys their Halloween is ruined."

When Mickey stepped foot back into the living room, he found his nephews rampaging, demanding a scary story. He tried to calm them down. "Boys, boys . . ."

Ferdie and Louie jumped up and down on the couch, pointing at Mickey. "Can't tell a scary story! Can't tell a scary story!"

The **laughing** and **taunting** continued, and Mickey just couldn't take it anymore.

"That's *it*! So! You don't think I can tell a story that'll scare the pants off ya, huh? Here we go! Once upon a time, there were **five rotten kids**. . . ."

In Mickey's latest story, the nephew characters **wreaked havoc** on innocent townsfolk.

"And they loved to steal pie! They stole from everyone. No pie was safe. The whole town was in an uproar. But the boys were too clever to be caught."

Back in Mickey's living room, the nephews were loving the story so far.

"Yeah!
Awesome!
Ha-ha!"

Mickey continued to tell his dark, twisted fairy tale.

"Every day was the same. Nothing ever changed. Until one day . . . a glorious scent came into their hideout."

A *purple wisp* of vapor wafted under the bridge, where it met the thieves.

"Pie!"

They rounded a corner and came upon an incredible pastry.

"'Twas the most *amazing* pie they had ever seen. They had to have it!"

The thieves' jaws dropped, and they drooled while a sweet old lady named Granny Hexobah pushed a cart with the magnificent pie.

"That's some pie you have there, Gramma."

Then the **devilish** boys stole her pie and triumphantly dashed off.

The boys **celebrated** their heist by eating the delicious pie. They wanted more, but they didn't know where Granny lived.

"Just then,
the amazing pie scent returned."

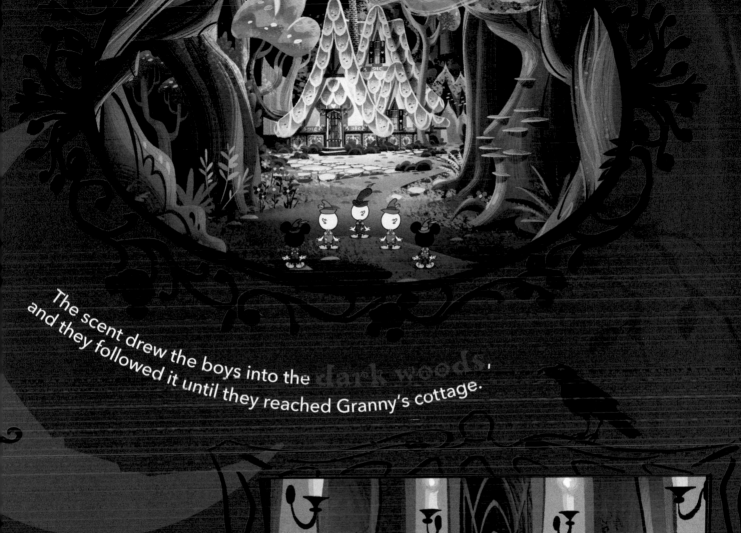

The scent drew the boys into the dark woods, and they followed it until they reached Granny's cottage.

They locked Granny out, and Huey formed a plan. "Those pies are here somewhere. Everybody split up."

The aroma led them through the dark, **creepy** cottage. Before they knew it, they started to get picked off one by one.

A painting came alive and yanked Morty inside the wall.

A bookshelf swept Louie away. **"Wa-ah!"**

A **dingy** cellar staircase turned into a slide, sending Dewey through a **trapdoor**.

"Yah-aahhh!"

Soon Ferdie disappeared into a black void, leaving Huey all alone and running for his life! Huey entered the kitchen and finally found a pie.

Entranced by it, he took a bite.

Huey froze as Granny Hexobah entered the kitchen.
"Well, well, well. Are you enjoying my pie? You really should try one fresh out of the oven."

She opened the oven door to reveal pies wearing the other boys' hats. Their faces pushed through the dough, pleading and whimpering.

Granny slammed the oven door shut. "Oh, not done yet. You must have guessed my secret ingredient."

"Little boys?"

"Oh, I don't just pick *any* little boys. I pick the most **snot-nosed**, rotten little boys I can find. And *you*, Huey, are the most rotten little boy I've come across!"

Granny laughed **maniacally** and suddenly turned into an **evil witch!** She grabbed her rolling pin.

"Let's bake some pies!"

Huey ran for his life as she chased him through the cottage.

Finally, he spotted the front door. "I'm free!"

But before he could escape, Granny grabbed him and yanked him back inside the cottage!

"There was no escape. Huey had become her next pie!"

The nephews were **scared to death**, and so were Goofy and Donald.

Mickey watched in satisfaction as everyone around him **panicked** and **rocketed** upstairs to cower under the blanket on his bed.

In the living room, he scooped up some Halloween candy and smiled. "Ha-ha, I knew I could tell a scary story! Another Halloween successfully put to bed.

You're welcome!"

The doorbell rang, and Mickey went to answer it. "Witches baking kids into pies! Scares 'em every time." But when Mickey opened the door, he found **Granny Hexobah** with a pie!

"Who wants PIE?"

Mickey **screamed** and zipped into the bed to hide with everyone else.

"That r-r-really was the ultimate scary story, Uncle Mickey."

"You want to hear another one?"

"NO!"

"G-g-good! Me neither!"

Granny Hexobah stood in the doorway as Daisy appeared at her side.

"Uh, what's up with Mickey?"

Granny **pulled off her head—** it was actually just Minnie with a mask on! "I don't know. Mickey usually *loves* my pie."